Puppy Power

by Judy Cox

illustrated by
Steve Björkman

SCHOLASTIC INC.
New York Toronto London Auckland Sydney
Mexico City New Delhi Hong Kong Buenos Aires

To my Reading Buddies
J. C.

ISBN-13: 978-0-545-11085-3
ISBN-10: 0-545-11085-8

12 11 10 9 8 7 6 5 4 3 2 1   8 9 10 11 12 13/0

Printed in the U.S.A.   40

First Scholastic printing, September 2008

Contents

Chapter 1

A Dead Toad

Fran saw a dead toad in the middle of the road. She sat back on her heels to look at it closely.

It was her favorite kind of roadkill. No blood. No guts. Nothing gooshy. She carefully peeled it off the pavement. It was as dry as an Egyptian mummy.

"Hey, you guys!" she yelled to the other kids waiting for the school bus. "Look at this!"

"Ugh," said Tiffanie. She tossed her shiny black hair. "Don't touch it. It's got germs."

Fran grinned.

"Here, Tiffanie! How about some tasty toasted toad guts?" Fran shoved the dead toad under Tiffanie's nose.

"Eeuw! No!" squealed Tiffanie. She waved it away.

Fran laughed. She loved teasing Tiffanie. She tossed the dead toad at her. "Tiffanie-Squiffanie! Catch!"

Tiffanie ducked. "I'm telling!" she yelled.

Fran laughed.

Just then something big ran down the street, headed right toward Fran. Something black. Something shaggy. Like a bear.

Someone yelled, "Stop!"

But the bear didn't stop. He knocked Fran down. He put his paws on Fran's shoulders. Something wet swiped her ear. His tongue was as big and wet as a washcloth.

"Hercules!" she yelled. "Get off!"

Fran gently shoved the bear away. It

wasn't really a bear. It was her black puppy, Hercules.

Hercules wagged his tail. His tongue hung out.

Hercules was only a puppy. A BIG puppy. Fran threw her arms around his neck and hugged him. His fur smelled like cocoa.

"What are you doing loose?" she asked him. "I thought Mom was walking you."

Hercules grinned. His leash trailed on the ground behind him. Fran grabbed the end.

Fran's mom came up, panting. "I don't know what we're going to do with this puppy," she said, shaking her head. She took the leash from Fran.

Fran didn't like the sound of that. But there was no time to ask Mom what she meant.

"Here comes the bus!" yelled Mark. All the kids ran to line up. Except Fran.

"See you later," said Mom. She kissed Fran good-bye and tugged Hercules down the street.

Fran hung back as the big yellow bus

growled to a stop. The doors slid open with a hiss. The rest of the kids got on.

Fran picked up the toad. She put it in her lunch box. You never knew when a dead toad might come in handy.

Chapter 2

Big-Foot Princess

"The end," said Miss Wilkins. She closed the fairy-tale book.

Fran yawned. Usually she liked listening to Miss Wilkins read. But today a warm spring breeze blew through the open window. It ruffled Miss Wilkins's brown curls. It tickled the back of Fran's neck. The breeze made Fran think of recess. Spring vacation. Summer. Anywhere but school!

"I have exciting news," said Miss Wilkins.

Fran sat up. She looked at Miss Wilkins. She liked her teacher. Most of the time.

What could the news be? A field trip?

"On Thursday we will hold tryouts for the third-grade play," continued Miss Wilkins. "This year we will present *Princess Penelope and the Pea*."

The Princess and the Pea! Fran loved the story of the princess who didn't look like a princess. It was Fran's favorite fairy tale.

"Me!" she yelled, waving her hand. "Pick me! I'll be Princess Penelope!"

"Who ever heard of a red-haired princess?" grumbled Tiffanie. Tiffanie sat behind Fran. She swung her perfect ponytail

7

and sniffed. "Who ever heard of a princess with big feet?"

Fran turned around in her seat. She narrowed her blue eyes. "For your information, my hair is not red," she told Tiffanie. She tossed her head. "It's strawberry blonde."

Tiffanie shrugged. "Whatever."

"And my feet are not big." Fran glanced down at her feet. Actually, she thought, they were pretty big. She stuck out her tongue. She crossed her eyes.

"Girls!" Miss Wilkins's voice sharpened. Fran knew that tone. Miss Wilkins was coming to the end of her rope.

Many times during the past school year Miss Wilkins had said: "Fran, I'm at the end of my rope with you."

Miss Wilkins certainly wouldn't pick her for Princess Penelope if she was at the end of her rope. Fran gave Miss Wilkins her nicest smile.

Miss Wilkins tapped the papers in her hand. "Tryouts will be at three o'clock tomorrow. Everyone will get a chance to read."

Then Miss Wilkins looked right at

Fran. "The teachers will decide who will be the best princess." She smiled. Her eyes crinkled up at the corners. "Besides, there are other parts."

Other parts, but only one princess, thought Fran. She didn't even hear Miss Wilkins give the math problems. She imagined herself onstage wearing a lacy pink dress. Saying her lines. Taking her bow. Everyone would clap. Everyone would say, "Hurray for Fran! The best princess ever!"

Chapter 3

The Boss of Tetherball

Fran jumped up when the recess bell rang. She shoved her math book inside her desk, crumpling her papers. She ran for the door. "Walk!" Miss Wilkins reminded her. But Fran didn't stop. She wanted to be first in line for tetherball.

A group of kindergartners stood by the hall door.

"Gangway!" she yelled. "Princess Fran coming through!" She pushed past. A little kid fell down, but Fran didn't stop. Why didn't he get out of her way? Kindergartners were just little squirts. What could they expect?

She raced to the tetherball. There was already a line. Mark was serving.

"Me first!" Fran yelled. She shoved to the front of the line, grabbed the ball, and swung.

"Hey!" yelled Allie. "No fair! You took cuts!"

Fran turned around. She narrowed her eyes. She put her fists on her hips. "So?" she asked in a hard voice. "Wanna make something of it?" That would fix Allie. Allie made a face. She walked away, muttering.

Two other kids left too. "I'm not playing with *her*," Fran heard one kid say. "She cheats."

Fran faced Mark. "You playing or not?" she asked.

Mark served. Fran grabbed the rope. She swung hard. The ball sailed over Mark's head. The rope wrapped around the pole.

"No ropers!" yelled Mark.

"You snooze, you lose!" Fran laughed. Mark scowled. He stomped off. "Poor sport!" Fran yelled after him.

She flexed her arms. She felt pumped up. Ready to roll.

"Next?" she called happily. But no one waited.

She brushed her hair out of her eyes. "I'll play by myself then," she muttered. *Thwack!* She punched the ball as hard as she could. The rope wrapped around the pole again and slowly unwound. "I'm the boss of tetherball!" she cried.

But tetherball wasn't much fun alone.

Across the playground she spotted a soccer game. Tiffanie, Kelsie, Caleb, and Eduardo raced after the black-and-white ball.

I'm way better than those guys, thought Fran.

She smacked the tetherball one last time. Then she ran across the playground. She'd show them. But as she reached the field, the bell rang. Fran skidded to a stop, her sneakers digging into the grass.

Just wait until next recess! She'd be the boss of soccer!

Mr. Brown, the recess duty teacher, stood by the door.

"Guess what?" Fran yelled. "The third grade is having a play, and I'm going to be Princess Penelope."

"Oh, she is not," said a voice behind her. "We haven't even had tryouts yet." Fran spun around. It was that know-it-all Tiffanie.

"Am too," said Fran. She put her hands on her hips.

"Are not," said Tiffanie. She stuck out her chin.

Fran stepped forward. Then she saw Mr. Brown watching. She took a step back.

"Okay," she said. "May the best princess win." Fran smiled sweetly as she watched Tiffanie walk down the hall.

Just wait until Tiffanie found that dead toad in her pretty pink backpack!

Chapter 4

Hercules

After school, Fran raced home from the bus stop. Before she could get through the gate to her front yard, something knocked her over.

"Hey!" she yelled. "Let me up!" Something heavy held her down. Something big. Something black. Something shaggy.

Hercules again!

She flung her arms around his neck. She buried her face in his thick fur. He licked

her ear with his big, pink tongue. "What are you doing out?" she asked. "Mom will have a fit."

Hercules grinned and wagged his tail.

Fran grabbed his collar. She opened the gate. She put him in the yard. Then she picked up her backpack and went inside.

"Mom!" Fran yelled.

"Up here," Mom called.

Fran flung her backpack on the floor. She pulled a crumpled note from Miss Wilkins out of her sweatshirt pocket. She knew it was about the dead toad Tiffanie found in her backpack.

She smoothed it out on the kitchen table. She glanced at the chart on the refrigerator. No star today. Well, it wasn't her fault! Tiffanie asked for it!

She grabbed a banana from the counter and pounded up the stairs to her room. Mom knelt in front of Fran's closet. A big cardboard box sat on the floor.

"I'm giving away old clothes," said Mom "Look at how short these pants are! And you need new shoes too. When are you going to stop growing, Frannie? When your head touches the ceiling?" She folded up a pair of jeans and put them into the box.

Fran laughed. She peeled the banana and bit off a chunk. She liked it when Mom teased.

Mom pushed herself up from the floor. She sat on Fran's bed. She patted the bedspread beside her. Fran sat next to Mom.

She rubbed Mom's round tummy. "Hello, baby!" she called. "Come out soon and play with me!"

Mom laughed. She put her arm around Fran.

"How did it go today?" she asked. "Was it a gold star day?"

Fran shook her head.

"Oh, Frannie," Mom said sadly. "You've got to try harder. You've got to think before you act."

"Look before you leap," said Fran. It was an old game.

"Watch before you wade," said Mom.

"Gaze before you gallop!" Fran laughed. But Mom didn't laugh this time.

"Hercules got out again," said Fran, biting another piece of banana. "I put him back in our yard."

Mom pushed her strawberry blonde hair out of her eyes. "Not again!" she said. "That's the third time this week. We can't have a dog that is out of control."

"But we'll keep him, won't we?" asked Fran anxiously. "He's a nice puppy, isn't he?"

"Yes, he's a nice puppy," Mom said. "He has a good heart. But he doesn't realize how big he is."

Mom shook her head. "And he's growing," she continued. "Newfoundlands get to be big, big dogs. If we can't control him now, I shudder to think what he will be like when he's fully grown!"

Mom rubbed her tummy. "I'll be busy when the baby comes. I can't take care of two babies at once. Hercules has to behave. Or else."

Fran swallowed the last bite of banana. She didn't want to hear that. "I can do it. I can make him behave."

Mom looked at Fran. "But you can't control your own behavior," she said sadly. "Maybe you aren't responsible enough for a puppy."

"Don't say that!" Fran pleaded. "Please say we'll keep him!" But Mom didn't answer.

Chapter 5

Tryouts

On Thursday at three o'clock, Fran burst out of class. She raced to the gym. Tryouts for the third-grade play were about to begin!

The gym swarmed with kids from every third-grade class. Like a beehive, thought Fran. And we are the bees. She signed up to read the part of Princess Penelope. Then she sat down on a bleacher to wait for her turn.

Lots of girls tried out for Princess Penelope. Fran watched closely. Some of them weren't bad, she had to admit. Mariah from Mrs. Rogers's class read nicely. So—unfortunately—did Amber. None of them is as good as I will be, thought Fran. But she couldn't stop her foot from jiggling nervously.

When it was her turn, Fran took a deep breath. She stood up straight and tall. She smiled sweetly at the third-grade teachers. She read her part in a loud, clear voice without missing even one word. She even twirled around on tippy toes to show how she would dance if *she* played the princess.

Next, Tiffanie read. Unfortunately, Tiffanie read beautifully. And she really looked like a princess with her long hair and her tiny feet. Fran chewed her lower lip. It would be hard to beat Tiffanie.

After everyone had tried out, Miss Wilkins stood up. She clapped her hands. Everyone stopped talking.

"Thank you all for coming," Miss Wilkins said. "You each did a fine job. Tonight the

teachers will decide who will play each part. We will hang up a cast list in the hall on Monday."

Fran grabbed her backpack. Monday! How could she ever wait until Monday?

Chapter 6

Reading Buddies

The next day was reading buddy day. All year Fran had been reading to a kinder-gartner named China. But last week China moved to Florida. Today Fran would get a new reading buddy. She wiggled impatiently as the third graders lined up. She poked Eduardo to make him walk faster.

Eduardo was from Mexico. He didn't speak much English yet. He turned around. "Hey!" he said. "No poosh."

Fran laughed. "No poosh," she teased. "You said 'No poosh'!"

Miss Wilkins put her hand on Fran's shoulder. "End of the line, Fran," she said.

"It's not fair!" said Fran. "It was a joke. Can't anyone take a joke?" She blew out a big, gusty sigh and went to the end of the line.

In the kindergarten room, the other third graders quickly found their reading buddies. They sat together in the beanbag chairs or on the rug. Fran stood alone.

Mr. Ellis, the kindergarten teacher, brought over a little boy.

"This is Jonathan," said Mr. Ellis with a smile. "He just moved here from Texas." He bent down. "Fran will be your reading buddy," he told Jonathan. Mr. Ellis walked away. He didn't see Jonathan stick out his tongue at Fran.

Fran folded her arms. She looked down at Jonathan. What a squirt, she thought. He had skinny little arms. He had skinny little legs in cowboy boots. His blond curls stuck up like feathers. He had a runny nose.

Fran took Jonathan by the hand. She led him to a beanbag chair. "Look what I brought," said Fran. She held out *Fox in Socks.*

Of course, she could read much harder books. She was probably the best reader in the whole third grade! During silent reading time, she was reading *Charlotte's Web.* But Miss Wilkins had told the class to choose short books to read to their buddies.

Jonathan wiped his nose on his shirttail. His T-shirt had pictures of ants and grasshoppers on the front. Bug Off, it read. Fran opened her book. She began to read.

She hadn't even finished the first page when Jonathan interrupted. "I don't like this story," he said. Even his voice sounded skinny.

Fran stopped reading. She looked at him. "Why not?"

Jonathan stuck out his lip. "I only like truck books." He got up. He started to walk away. "I want to go home," he said. "I don't like foxes, and I don't like you."

Fran didn't have a truck book. "Come

back here," she told him. "You have to lis-
ten to me read."

"No," said Jonathan. "You're not the boss
of me."

"I am too," said Fran. She glared at him, upset and worried. She didn't want Jonathan to leave. She was supposed to read to him for twenty minutes. What would Miss Wilkins say?

"I'm the reading buddy boss," Fran told him. China never did this kind of stuff. China liked being read to. Jonathan should too. He should behave.

To stop him from leaving, Fran reached out and yanked Jonathan's wrist. Jonathan tumbled backward into the beanbag. He began to howl.

"She pushed me!" he yelled. "She pushed me!"

Fran stood up, outraged. "I did not!" All the third graders and their kindergarten reading buddies stared. Fran stared back uncomfortably. If Miss Wilkins walked in now, Fran figured she could kiss the role of Princess Penelope good-bye.

Jonathan threw himself to the floor. He screwed up his eyes. Tears ran down his cheeks. His face turned red.

"I don't like you," he sobbed. "You're mean!"

"I didn't—," Fran started to say, but it was too late. Miss Wilkins was marching over, and she looked as if she was at the end of her rope.

That afternoon Fran leaned against the brick wall of the school. Time out, again! Sometimes she felt as if she'd spent the whole of third grade against the wall.

This time it was all Jonathan's fault. Now she didn't get recess! No chance to beat Mark at tetherball. No chance to prove she was the boss of soccer. She looked down at her new, shiny-silver sneakers. They had little red lights on the sides. Lights that twinkled when she ran. Now she had no chance to run and show them off.

And Miss Wilkins said she was skating

on thin ice, whatever that meant. Fran wasn't sure, but it sounded a lot like Miss Wilkins was at the end of her rope. At least she didn't say Fran couldn't be considered for Princess Penelope!

The door around the corner creaked open. Two grown-ups came out talking.

They couldn't see her. She couldn't see them. It sounded like Miss Wilkins and Mr. Brown.

"I'm worried," said Miss Wilkins. (If it *was* Miss Wilkins.) "There's a girl in my class who is really talented and bright. But her rude behavior puts off the other children." Fran leaned closer, listening hard.

Mr. Brown laughed. "I know who you mean," he said. "'The tetherball boss.' She'll never make friends that way. What do you

suppose it'll take for her to change?" The door opened again and all was quiet. They must have gone inside.

Fran slumped against the wall. "The tetherball boss." They couldn't be talking about her, could they? Talented? Bright? No friends?

She shook her head. No way. Must be someone else. But a little worry gnawed at her, like a worm inside an apple.

Chapter 7

Puppy Kindergarten

That night Fran set the table for dinner.

"Ten more minutes," said Mom. Her face shone pink from the heat of the oven. "Go tell Dad."

Fran went into the family room. Dad sat on the couch, folding the laundry. Hercules lay on the rug, chewing on a leather bone. He rolled his eyes when he saw Fran.

Fran flopped down next to Hercules. She lay on her back. She waved her feet in the air. She turned them this way and that. Looking at them. Wondering.

"Tiffanie said my feet are too big," she said.

"Let me see those dogs," said Dad. He sat on the floor beside her. He took Fran's foot in his hand. He pulled off her shoe. He waved his hand in front of his nose, pretending to faint from the smell.

"Whoa," he said. He pulled off her sock. "Frannie, you're growing; you need big feet. Some people say you can tell how big a dog will be by the size of its paws when it is a puppy."

He tickled her foot until she squealed. "Judging by the size of these, I'd say you'll grow up to be a Saint Bernard at least!"

Fran grinned. Then she frowned. "But do you think I can still be a princess? All the princesses I've seen have little feet. Like Cinderella."

"Of course you can be a princess. You'll always be *my* princess," said Dad. He ruffled her hair.

Fran sighed. She liked being Dad's princess, but she wanted to be Princess Penelope. Princess of the third-grade play!

"Dinner!" called Mom. "Come and get it!"

Hercules's ears went up. He jumped up. His body tensed.

"WOOF!" he barked.

Hercules raced for the kitchen. His paws skidded on the bare floor. Thump! He hit the table. Crash! Plates and silverware slid to the floor. Splash! Milk dripped from an overturned glass. The meat platter sailed across the table. It landed on the floor.

"My roast chicken!" cried Mom.

Hercules gobbled it up.

Mom put her hands on her hips. "That's it," she said. "I've had it with that dog. Either he gets trained or he's out of here."

Fran's eyes filled with tears. They couldn't give Hercules away! She grabbed his collar. She tugged him away from the mess.

Dad looked at Fran. He looked at Hercules. "Saturday," he said. "Puppy kindergarten for you!"

* * *

On Saturday Fran and Dad took Hercules to puppy kindergarten.

The dog trainer, Mr. Marcos, met them at the door. He was a small man with a big black mustache. Fran thought it looked like a woolly bear caterpillar under his nose.

"Welcome," he told them.

The room looked like a small gym. Puppies of all sizes played together in the center of the floor. A row of chairs stood against the wall. Fran sat down next to Dad.

The room swarmed with dogs. Big dogs, little dogs. Dogs with floppy ears, dogs with tall ears. Dogs with short tails, dogs with long tails. Even a dog with a tail curled over its back.

Fran thought she'd never seen so many different kinds of dogs in her life.

One little puppy hid under a chair. All Fran could see was a quivering black nose.

"Come out, Suzie," coaxed a lady in a flowered hat. But Suzie wouldn't come out. She wouldn't behave.

Just like Jonathan, thought Fran.

"Now I know why they call it puppy kindergarten," she whispered to Dad.

Hercules shook his big black head. His ears flopped. He didn't like wearing a leash. He wanted to play. Dad unsnapped his leash. Hercules bounded into the mass of puppies. Soon he was romping. Rolling on his back. Play-biting. Growling softly.

But then playtime ended. "Leash your dogs," said Mr. Marcos. Hercules didn't want to stop. Dad held him while Fran snapped on his leash. When all the puppies were with their owners, class began.

First, Mr. Marcos showed the owners how to teach their puppies to come when called.

"Now let's practice," he told them. "Fran, would you and Hercules come here?"

Mr. Marcos told Fran to stand on one side of the room. Dad stood across the room with Hercules. Mr. Marcos handed Fran a tiny bit of freeze-dried liver. He showed her how to give it to Hercules when he came.

"Come here, Hercules," called Fran.

At first Hercules didn't want to come. He wanted to snuffle the other puppies. Over and over they practiced. Each time Hercules bounded over to Fran, she gave him a treat. She gave him a hug and a pat too. Soon he came every time she called him.

Next, Mr. Marcos showed Fran how to signal Hercules to sit, stand, and lie down. It was hard to get Hercules to sit because he was so big. Mr. Marcos and Dad had to help. But finally Hercules did what she told him.

"Hercules wants to please you," Mr. Marcos said.

Fran smiled. She gave Hercules a hug.

He licked her ear. Mr. Marcos continued. "Hercules is a beautiful puppy. But if you want his behavior to change, you must practice! So now you have homework. Practice twenty, thirty times every day!"

Mr. Marcos clapped his hands. "That's it for today," he said. "Next week I will show you how to train your puppies to heel."

Dad snapped Hercules's leash onto his collar. Hercules pulled away. He didn't want to go. He wanted to follow the other puppies. He wanted to play.

"Sit," said Dad in a firm voice. Hercules sat down. He sighed. He rolled his eyes.

Fran laughed. Hercules looked so sad. "I guess he likes recess better than school," said Fran. "But he sat when you told him to! He can behave when he tries!"

Chapter 8

Gangway for the Princess

On Monday Fran got to school before the first bell. She pulled open the heavy front door. Her heart pounded in her chest. Even though she had told Mom and Dad that she was sure to get the part, she still worried. What if the third-grade teachers didn't want a princess with red hair? What if they didn't want a princess with big feet?

What if they picked *Tiffanie*?

A group of noisy kids clustered around

the bulletin board. Fran elbowed her way to the front.

"Gangway!" she hollered. "Coming through!" She bumped Mariah and Amber aside. She planted herself squarely in front. Her eyes searched the list.

There! At the very top!

"Princess Penelope—Fran Beatty," she read out loud.

"YES!" she shouted. "I'm the best!" She pumped her fist in the air.

A hand fell on her shoulder. Fran stopped chanting and looked up. Miss Wilkins towered above her. She crooked her finger. "Come with me," she said.

Fran followed Miss Wilkins down the hall to the third-grade classroom. Miss Wilkins folded her arms. She leaned against her desk. Fran searched her face for clues. Was Miss Wilkins mad? Was she at the end of her rope?

But Miss Wilkins smiled. "Fran," she said. "The other teachers and I agreed you gave the best reading. Your voice was clear and strong. You looked happy and confident.

You stood up straight, like a princess. I'm proud of you, Fran. You did a super job."

Fran beamed.

Then Miss Wilkins lowered her voice. She leaned close. "But, Fran. A princess needs to act like a princess. Even at recess. No pushing. No teasing. No bossing. No roughhousing. One step out of line and you are out of the play."

Fran blinked. Out of the play? She suddenly remembered overhearing the teachers at recess. *Talented and bright. But her rude behavior puts off the other children.* A horrible thought struck her. What if Miss Wilkins asked Tiffanie to play Princess Penelope?

Miss Wilkins tapped her fingers, waiting for Fran to say something.

"Okay," said Fran. "Sure. No problem." She nodded, but inside she felt worried and uncertain.

Miss Wilkins smiled again. She put her hand on Fran's shoulder. She gave a little squeeze. "I knew I could count on you."

Fran stood for a moment, watching Miss Wilkins walk back behind her desk.

Fran let out her breath. No way would she let Tiffanie-Squiffanie have *her* part!

That afternoon Fran sprawled on her bed. She was supposed to pick up her clothes. She was supposed to make her bed. She was supposed to practice with Hercules.

But she lay on her stomach with her feet in the air. She opened her book. She wanted to finish *Charlotte's Web* before dinner. Hercules pushed open her door. He put his cold nose right in her face. His tongue came out. He gave her a lick.

"Hercules!" she yelled, shoving him away. He sat back on his haunches. His mouth stretched wide, his tongue out, grinning.

She couldn't help herself. She grinned back.

She closed her book. She couldn't read with Hercules licking her. She swung her feet over the edge of the bed. "Help me make my bed," she ordered.

Hercules wagged his tail. He grabbed the edge of her bedspread as she tried to smooth it out. She pulled. He tugged. She pulled harder. Hercules growled and shook the bedspread.

This was getting nowhere! Hercules might rip the bedspread! Fran let go of it so it wouldn't tear. She flopped down on the floor.

Hercules pushed his nose under her arm. She scratched behind his ears. His tail thumped the floor.

She spotted the cardboard box of old clothes. Something pink caught her eye.

Fran dug through the box. Mom must have cleaned out her own closet too. In the bottom of the box Fran found a pink dress.

She pulled it out and held it up.

A party dress of Mom's!

She quickly pulled it over her shorts and T-shirt.

She looked in the mirror.

A vision in pink stared back.

"Princess Penelope?" said Fran. "Is that you?" She smiled and curtsied to her reflection. "At your service, Your Highness."

She hummed a little tune and spun around on her tippy toes. She brushed her strawberry blonde hair out of her eyes. She looked like a real princess! The long dress even covered up her big feet!

"Dance with me, Prince Hercules," she ordered. She picked up Hercules's front paws. She held them in her hands. He balanced on his back feet. Step, step. She looked at them waltzing in the mirror and laughed. Hercules rolled his big brown eyes. He let out a gusty sigh. He didn't seem to enjoy dancing.

"Okay," she said. "No more dancing. You have my royal permission to sit the next one out." She hummed. She twirled to make the dress fluff out.

Hercules snapped at the ruffles. "Stop it, Hercules!" ordered Fran. "You'll tear it."

Hercules wagged his tail harder. He whined. He tugged the ruffles again. He thought it was a game.

Fran swept the dress out of his reach. What had Mr. Marcos said? Be firm? Make him mind?

"SIT!" she ordered in her bossiest playground voice.

To her surprise, Hercules sat. He cocked his head. He put up his ears. His tongue hung out, but his eyes were sad. He wanted to play. Not sit.

"Good dog," said Fran. She patted his head. "Come on. Let's go do your homework. I can dress up later."

She dropped the princess dress on the floor. She and Hercules bounded down the stairs. Plenty of time to be a princess later. Right now, she and Hercules had better practice. She wanted to show Mom what a good puppy he could be!

Chapter 9

Gold Star Day

The next morning Fran pounded down the stairs to the kitchen. She didn't want to miss the bus.

Dad stood at the kitchen counter. He set out two lunch boxes. One for Fran. One for Dad. He spread peanut butter on a slice of bread. "Tuna or peanut butter, Frannie?" he asked.

"Peanut butter," said Fran. "With honey and raisins. On wheat." Her favorite.

Dad always made sandwiches in the morning before leaving for his job as manager of the hardware store.

Mom worked on weekends as a nurse's aide. She had weekdays off. This morning she sat at the table, eating oatmeal. She propped her feet on a chair. Fran knew she sat that way because her ankles hurt. Sometimes they swelled up. All because of the baby!

Fran pulled out a bowl and a box of cereal. She slammed them on the counter. The dishes rattled.

"Slow down," said Mom, rubbing her forehead. She sounded cranky in the mornings. The baby again, of course!

Fran tried to pour her cereal quietly. She spilled a little milk. Hercules lapped it up.

"What's up for today?" asked Dad.

Fran paused, her spoon halfway to her mouth. "Reading buddy day again. Can I stay home? I can help Mom."

"Stay home?" said Dad. "But you love to read!" He opened two slices of bread like a book and pretended to read.

Fran didn't laugh. "I wish I didn't have Jonathan for a partner. He won't behave. When I try to make him, Miss Wilkins gets mad."

"Maybe you should make friends with Jonathan," said Dad. "He probably doesn't have many friends yet."

Fran thought. Then she raced upstairs to get a book from her shelf. She stuffed it in her backpack.

After breakfast Fran fed Hercules. First she made him sit down. Otherwise he would knock her over when she tried to fill his dish.

"Sit!" she told him firmly. "Stay!" Hercules sat. He was getting pretty good!

She scooped kibbles out of a huge blue bag. She poured them in his dish.

"Hercules, come," she called when his dish was full. Hercules bounded over. He wolfed down his food.

"Look!" yelled Fran. "Hercules is behaving!"

"Good job, Fran," said Dad. "It's all that practice."

"Now can we keep him?" She looked at Mom.

Mom rubbed her ankles. "We'll see," she said.

Fran wasn't giving up. "Can I take him to the park after school?" she asked. "We can practice there."

Mom looked up and smiled. "The fresh air and exercise will be good for both of you," she said.

"Time to go," said Dad. "You don't want to miss the bus on reading buddy day."

Fran grabbed her lunch box. She stuffed it in her backpack. "Bye, Mom!" She flung her arms around Mom. She kissed Mom. "Bye, Dad!" She gave Dad a kiss and a hug too.

"Have a gold star day, Frannie!" said Mom.

"Think before you tread!" said Dad. "Peer before you pounce!"

"Look before I leap! I know! I know!" said Fran. "I will!" She ran down the side-walk to the bus stop.

That afternoon Fran walked down the hall with the other third graders. Fran hoped Jonathan would be absent. She crossed her fingers. If Jonathan was absent, she could read by herself. She could finish *Charlotte's Web*.

Mr. Ellis met the third graders by the door. Fran's heart sank when she saw him holding Jonathan's hand.

Today Jonathan wore a T-shirt that read Is it Recess Yet? And cowboy boots, of course.

"Hi," said Fran. She tried to use her quiet voice. She didn't want to scare him. Miss Wilkins might be watching.

But her quiet voice didn't work on Jonathan. He folded his arms and stuck out his bottom lip.

"I couldn't find a truck book," she said. Jonathan's face began to crumple.

"Don't cry!" said Fran. If he cried, it would be Hello, Miss Wilkins and Goodbye, Princess Penelope.

"I brought this," Fran said quickly. She

held out a red book. *"Mike Mulligan and His Steam Shovel*. It's almost a truck book."

Jonathan looked at the steam shovel on the cover. He stopped frowning. He narrowed his eyes. He nodded slowly. Fran breathed a sigh of relief.

Fran and Jonathan sat in a beanbag chair. Fran opened the book and began to read. As she read him the story about Mike and Mary Anne, Jonathan started to smile.

Jonathan pointed to a dog in the picture. "My favorite kind of dog is a collie dog," he said. "You know that kind?"

"Sure," said Fran. "My favorite kind of dog is a Newfie."

"What's a Newfie?" Jonathan wiped his nose on his sleeve.

"A Newfoundland. A big, black, water dog. They're heroes. They can rescue swimmers who get lost at sea."

"I've never seen that kind of dog," said Jonathan. He frowned. "Are you pretending?"

"No, really," said Fran. "I have a Newfie puppy. His name is Hercules."

Jonathan's face lit up. "Hey! I want to see that dog! Bring him to my house."

"Good idea," said Fran. "Maybe you could meet me in the park instead. Ask your mom."

Her heart felt light as she waved good-bye to Jonathan and lined up at the door. That Jonathan kid was okay after all. She had won over her reading buddy. She had a friend.

Chapter 10

"You big bully!"

When Fran got home from play practice, she found Mom cleaning out the kitchen cupboards. Boxes, cans, and bottles covered the counters. Mom wore a bandanna over her hair.

"What's up, buttercup?" asked Mom.

"Gold star day!" Fran said. Mom was so big that it was hard to hug her. She patted Mom's tummy. "Hi, baby!"

"Congratulations!" Mom handed Fran a

gold star from the box on top of the fridge. Fran stuck it on her chart. She pounded it down with her fist. That would hold it good and tight.

Fran peeled the wrapper from a granola bar. She took a bite. She yanked Hercules's leash from the peg on the door.

"Can I take Hercules to the park now?"

Mom tucked a lock of hair under her bandanna. "Be back before dinnertime."

Fran shoved open the back door. "Gangway for Princess Penelope!" she shouted.

Hercules lay on the dirt under the maple tree, chewing on a rubber bone. "Hercules!" called Fran. "Come here, boy!"

Hercules bounded over. He looked as if he might jump up and knock her down.

"SIT!" yelled Fran in her bossy voice.

Hercules skidded to a stop. He sat. He didn't jump up. "Good boy," she said. She patted his thick black fur. He licked her hand.

"Mom!" called Fran. "Look at Hercules! He's doing well, isn't he?"

Mom stood in the doorway. She smiled. "Sure, honey."

"So we can keep him?"

"We'll see," said Mom.

That again! Fran didn't want to hear it. She wanted Mom to say they would never ever get rid of a wonderful puppy like Hercules!

"Time for a walk," Fran said. She snapped the leash on his collar. "Homework time! You want a gold star at puppy kindergarten, don't you?"

The park was three blocks away. Hercules tugged on the leash.

When they reached the park, Fran heard a voice say, "Hey!" She turned around. Jonathan stood on the sidewalk, holding his mom's hand. Fran grinned, surprised at how glad she was to see him. It was good to have a friend, even if he was only a kindergartner.

"Is this your dog?" Jonathan squatted down. He put out one finger. He touched Hercules. "Nice doggy," he said.

"His name is Hercules," Fran said. She used her quiet voice with Jonathan every time now.

"Can I pet him?"
"Yeah," said Fran. "Go ahead."

After Jonathan petted Hercules, Fran said, "We have to practice now. I'm teaching Hercules good manners."

Fran and Hercules walked to the grass. She felt important as she worked with Hercules. "Sit," she told him. "Come!" Hercules bounded over, and she gave him a doggy treat. "Stay," she said.

They practiced until the five-o'clock whistle sounded at the sugar beet factory.

Fran blew the hair out of her hot, sweaty face. Man, she was hot! She needed a drink. She tied Hercules to the bike rack and ran to the drinking fountain.

A long line curled down the sidewalk. Little kids! They were sooooo slow. Fran lined up at the end, behind Jonathan. "Hurry up!" she said.

"Don't push," someone said.

The line took forever. Fran jiggled from side to side impatiently. "Can't you hustle?" she snapped.

Finally, only Jonathan was ahead of her. He stood on tiptoe. He took a long, slow sip. If he didn't hurry up, she'd be late getting home. She might even get grounded. Mom might say she wasn't responsible enough for a puppy.

"MOVE IT, SQUIRT!" Fran shouted. She forgot all about using a quiet voice. She gave Jonathan a little shove to speed him up.

"OW!"

Jonathan turned around, his hand over

his mouth. Blood dripped between his fingers and ran down his chin. He'd cut his lip on the fountain.

Fran stared in horror. She'd never meant to hurt him. She reached out to comfort him, but he pulled away.

"I hate you!" he yelled. Tears streamed down his face. Jonathan ran to his mom.

Fran ran after him. "I'm sorry!" she

yelled. "It was an accident!" But she knew it wasn't really. She knew the exact moment she'd decided to speed him up with a little shove. She never thought he'd get hurt.

Jonathan buried his head in his mom's lap and sobbed. Fran felt awful. She watched helplessly as Jonathan's mom held a tissue to his mouth to stop the bleeding. His mom glared at Fran.

"Don't you know how to behave?" she snapped. She picked up Jonathan in her arms.

"You big bully!" yelled Jonathan over her shoulder. They left the park.

Fran's head spun. What had Jonathan called her?

A *bully*?

In a daze, Fran untied Hercules. She let him pull her down the sidewalk.

They flew home. Fran unsnapped his leash. Hercules followed her into the kitchen.

"Frannie," said Mom. "You're just in time to set the table."

Fran didn't answer. She pounded up the

stairs to her room. She didn't even notice Hercules following. She slammed her bedroom door and stared into her mirror.

Her face stared back, pinched and white. Her freckles stood out like red dots.

"I didn't mean it," she whispered. She remembered Jonathan's pale face. His tears. The blood. What if he'd knocked out a tooth? Her eyes filled with tears. She hoped he hadn't knocked out a tooth.

He called her a bully. She wiped her eyes.

"I'm not a bully," she whispered. "I'm not. I'm funny! I'm the boss of tetherball! I'm the best reader in the whole third grade. I'm Princess Penelope."

She wasn't a bully! Bullies were mean! She wasn't mean.

She stared at her face in the mirror.

She remembered putting the dead toad in Tiffanie's backpack. Maybe that was kind of mean. But it was Tiffanie's fault! If Tiffanie hadn't bugged her, Fran wouldn't need to do it. She had to stick up for herself!

Didn't she?

She remembered yelling at Rebecca on the swings. But that wasn't being a bully. Rebecca was supposed to get off when Fran counted one hundred hippopotamuses. Rebecca was a crybaby.

Wasn't she?

She remembered Eduardo's face when she teased him about his English. Wasn't she just being funny?

Maybe it wasn't funny if someone ended up in tears.

She remembered cheating at tetherball, and bossing, and pushing, and teasing. All the times someone had been hurt, or embarrassed, or scared by the things she'd done.

Oh, my gosh, thought Fran. It's true. I am a bully.

The face in the mirror crumpled. Tears dripped down Fran's cheeks. She flung herself on her bed, kicking the pink Princess Penelope dress to the floor. She buried her face in her pillow.

Hercules put his cold nose in her hand as if to comfort her. But Fran didn't even feel it.

Chapter 11

Gaze Before You Gallop

The first thing Fran saw when she woke up the next morning was the princess dress. It lay in a heap on the floor where she had kicked it the day before.

She snatched it up. She crumpled it into a ball. She flung it across the room. She hated it. It reminded her of yesterday. But then she picked it up and shook it out. She hung it in her closet. It wasn't the dress's fault.

Hercules bounded up the stairs. He rushed in, about to jump on her. "Sit!" she told him firmly.

He skidded to a stop and sat. He looked at her, his head cocked, his ears perked up.

Fran looked at him. He rolled his eyes. His tongue came out, and he grinned at her. He didn't jump up. He didn't put his big paws on her shoulders. He didn't lick her face. He didn't knock her down.

What a change! She remembered the rowdy puppy who chewed, and bit, and jumped, and ran.

If Hercules could change, so could she.

She dressed quickly and ran downstairs for breakfast. She was not a bully! She'd show them all!

At school Fran didn't run to be first in line like she usually did. She made herself hold the door open and let everyone else go ahead. Eduardo turned around and smiled.

"*Gracias,*" he said.

A glow warmed Fran. She smiled back. Piece of cake! This wasn't so hard after all!

But it *was* awfully hard. Over the next few weeks, her resolve was tested every day.

On Tuesday Rebecca wouldn't give up the swing. Not even when Fran counted to one hundred. Fran clenched her fists, determined not to yell.

On Wednesday Mark beat her at tetherball. Fran ground a little piece of dirt down into dust with the heel of her shoe. But she didn't cheat.

On Thursday she let Kelsie go ahead of

her at the drinking fountain. Even though Fran got there first.

On Friday Tiffanie whispered, "Frannie, Frannie, underpanty." Fran's face turned red. She clenched her fists. She wanted to smack that smart-aleck Tiffanie-Squiffanie into next Tuesday!

She closed her eyes. Quick! What would Hercules do? Fran imagined Hercules wearing the princess dress and waltzing with a poodle. Fran laughed out loud; and when she opened her eyes, Tiffanie was gone.

Fran sighed with relief when the bell rang. For the first time in her life, she was glad recess was over.

Mr. Brown stood at the school door. "Way to go, Princess Fran!" he said. "You stayed out of trouble all week. Give me five." He held out his palm. Fran slapped it.

"Thank you, Mr. Brown," Fran said. She shoved her hair out of her eyes. "Being a princess is harder than it looks, you know."

* * *

The next week Fran saw Jonathan playing by himself on the monkey bars. She waved. But Jonathan ran away. Fran blinked back tears. Would he ever forgive her?

That afternoon when rehearsal ended, Miss Wilkins called Fran over. "I've seen a definite improvement in your behavior, Fran," she said. "Good job!"

Fran smiled, glad her teacher had noticed. But then she bit her lip. "Jonathan won't play with me," she said.

"Give it some time," said Miss Wilkins. "Remember, Rome wasn't built in a day."

Fran nodded. But she sighed as she walked to the school bus.

The days dragged on. It was just like the series of tests Princess Penelope had to go through, thought Fran. Without Hercules to play with at home and the rehearsals for *Princess Penelope and the Pea* after school, she couldn't have stood it.

The hardest test came at lunch a week before the play opened.

Every Tuesday Fran helped Mrs. Ellen, the lunch lady. Fran wore plastic gloves and a shower cap over her hair. She wore a white plastic apron. Her job was to hand out milk cartons.

Fran loved being a lunch helper. She liked leaving Miss Wilkins's class at the first bell. She liked the way the cold milk cartons felt as she plopped them on the trays.

Fran rubbed her forehead with the back of her gloved hand. The cafeteria was hot.

The line of kids snaked through the cafeteria. She gave milk to Eduardo and said *"De nada"* when he said *"Gracias."* She gave milk to Rebecca and didn't slam it down on the tray like she used to. She gave milk to Kelsie and Caleb and Amber and Ramon.

She finished the third graders. Next, the kindergartners lined up. They looked tiny. Fran handed milk to Elizabeta, Miriam, Julian, Denton, and Carla. She smiled and said "Hi" to everyone. She realized with surprise that she knew all the kindergartners by name. They weren't just little squirts after all.

Jonathan was the last in line. She set his milk on his tray. It had been weeks since that day in the park. On reading buddy days he barely spoke to her. Had he forgiven her yet?

"Hey," she said softly, so she wouldn't scare him. "Wanna come to my house and play with my dog?"

Jonathan looked at her. Would he smile, or would he cry? Worse, would he call her a bully in front of everyone? He wiped his nose with the back of his hand.

Just then a big kid—a fifth grader named Len—raced up. "Hey, you!" he yelled at Fran. "Milk! Give me milk! I'm dying of thirst here."

He shoved Jonathan. "Outta the way, twerp."

Jonathan stumbled. He tripped over his cowboy boots. His tray flew out of his

hands. It crashed to the floor. Green beans, mashed potatoes, and hamburger gravy covered him from head to toe.

Jonathan's face crumpled. Tears spurted from his eyes. He howled.

"Hey, Len!" yelled Fran. "What do you think you're doing, you big meanie?" She wanted to leap over the milk cart and thump him. He shouldn't treat a little kid like that!

Fran ran around the milk cart. Her hands balled into fists. Len walked away laughing. None of the teachers had seen him. She longed to kick him in the behind. Serve him right!

She stopped short. She seemed to hear voices in her head. First came Dad's voice saying, "Look before you leap."

Then she heard Mom say, "Have a gold star day!"

Mr. Marcos said, "Practice, practice, practice."

And finally Miss Wilkins said, "Behave like a princess."

Fran gave a long, gusty sigh. She rolled

her eyes just like Hercules did when she made him heel. She didn't kick that big kid Len. She didn't knock him down, or punch him, or call him names.

Even though she really, really wanted to.

Fran pushed her strawberry blonde hair out of her eyes. She knelt down next to Jonathan. She gave him a crumpled tissue from her pocket. He blew his nose.

Fran helped Mrs. Ellen wipe gravy off the floor. She helped wipe mashed potatoes off Jonathan.

"I'll get you a new tray," she told him. He stopped crying and sniffed.

Fran peeled off her plastic gloves. She took Jonathan's hand and led him to a table. She got him a new tray of food. She got him a new carton of milk.

"Good job, Fran," said Mrs. Ellen. "We're done. You can go eat now."

Fran took her tray next to Jonathan. He gave her a watery smile. She told him stories about Hercules while he ate. Soon he stopped sniffling and laughed.

"Can I come over today and play with your puppy?" he asked.

"Yeah," she said, grinning. "You bet!"

Chapter 12

The Play

On the night of the third-grade play, Fran waited backstage. She pulled open the curtain to peek at the audience. An excited buzz filled the gym as people found their seats and sat down. Folding chairs had been set up for the audience. The gym was nearly full. Probably everyone in town wanted to see *Princess Penelope and the Pea!*

Mom and Dad sat in the front row. Miss

Wilkins sat behind them. Too bad Hercules couldn't come too. But dogs weren't allowed at plays. Not even well-behaved dogs.

Last Saturday had been the last day of puppy kindergarten. Now Hercules could heel, stay, and sit. He came when called. He stopped jumping up on people. He even stayed inside the yard while Fran was at school. He lay in the shade under a tree, gnawing his rubber bone until she came home.

Last night at dinner Fran had asked, "Can we keep him?"

Mom smiled. "Yes, Fran," she said. "We can keep him."

Hercules had heard his name and thumped his tail. Mom nodded. "He's learned to behave. And so have you, Fran. We're proud of you."

Fran grinned. Gold stars filled the chart on the fridge.

Now, behind the curtain, Fran swallowed hard. She knew all her lines. She knew all her moves. But would she remember? Her stomach fluttered with butterflies.

She smoothed the pink ruffles of Mom's party dress. She straightened the sparkly crown on her head.

The play began. Fran remembered all her lines. She said them loudly and confidently, like a true princess. She danced on the tippy toes of her beautiful big feet. She smiled and held her crowned head high.

There was only one glitch. Tiffanie, who played a lady-in-waiting, tripped on the hem of her long blue dress. The old Fran would have pointed and laughed. The new Fran helped Tiffanie to her feet.

At the play's end, Fran heard the applause and went out front with the others to take a final bow. Dad sat in the front row, grinning and clapping. Mom sat next to him, wiping her eyes. Was she laughing or crying? It was hard to tell. Miss Wilkins gave Fran a thumbs-up.

Fran took a deep breath and let out a gusty sigh. She took Tiffanie's hand and the hand of the boy who played the prince. The whole cast raised their hands and bowed together.

Then Fran stepped to the front of the stage alone, as Miss Wilkins had taught her. Her heart still pounded. Her cheeks ached from smiling. But now she grinned with satisfaction. She crossed one foot behind her, held her frilly pink skirt out, and curtsied. Deep and low. Like a real princess.

Then she clasped her hands over her head and shook them, like a champion boxer. Princess Fran! The best princess ever!

Fran's Notes on Puppy Training

It is a good idea to take your puppy to puppy kindergarten. You will learn so much! They even let kids come, as long as a grown-up comes too. But if you can't take your puppy to kindergarten, there are books and videos at the library that will help you learn what to do.

Here are some of the things Hercules and I learned to do at puppy kindergarten.

The first things you will learn are how to train your dog to come, to sit, and to stay. Your puppy should learn to come when you call, so it won't chase cars or squirrels. Or it might get lost if it runs away.

Here is how to do it. Call your puppy. Then say, "Good dog," and give it a pat on the head and a treat. You have to practice this many times every day.

Mr. Marcos showed me how to train Hercules to sit. First I called him to me. Then I gave him a pat and a doggie treat. I touched his collar and said, "SIT," in a firm voice. I used my bossy playground voice. It is all right to use it with dogs, just not with people.

At first Hercules wouldn't sit, so Dad pushed his rear end down. Then Hercules sat and I gave him a doggie treat, and said, "Good dog." It is important to tell your dog when it is doing well.

To teach your puppy to stay, first call it. When it comes, say, "Good dog," and give your puppy a treat. Then tell your puppy to sit and give it a treat. Put your hand up, with the palm facing out, and say, "STAY," in your playground voice. Mr. Marcos said it is hard for puppies to hear children's voices, so you have to be LOUD. That is not a problem for me! I am the boss of LOUD!

Next, you walk away. Do not let the puppy follow. If it does, start over. Do not give your puppy a treat until it can stay and wait for you to call. Believe me, it will take A LOT of practice!

One of the next things I learned was to train Hercules to heel. That was great, because then he did not pull on the leash anymore! And just in time too, because now that my little baby sister is finally born, I am in charge of walking Hercules every single day.

To teach Hercules to heel, Mr. Marcos had me hold my left hand down by my side with a treat hidden in it. Hercules could smell the treat but not eat it. Not yet. Then I walked around the room, calling him to follow me. We practiced turning, and Hercules had to stay on my left side. We practice when I take him to the park to play with Jonathan.

Hercules is getting so good at following commands that I am planning to enter him in a dog show next month! And I just know that we are going to WIN!